HELLO NINJA

Hello Georgie

By N. D. Wilson Illustrated by Forrest Dickison

HARPER

An Imprint of HarperCollinsPublishers

Hello, ninja.

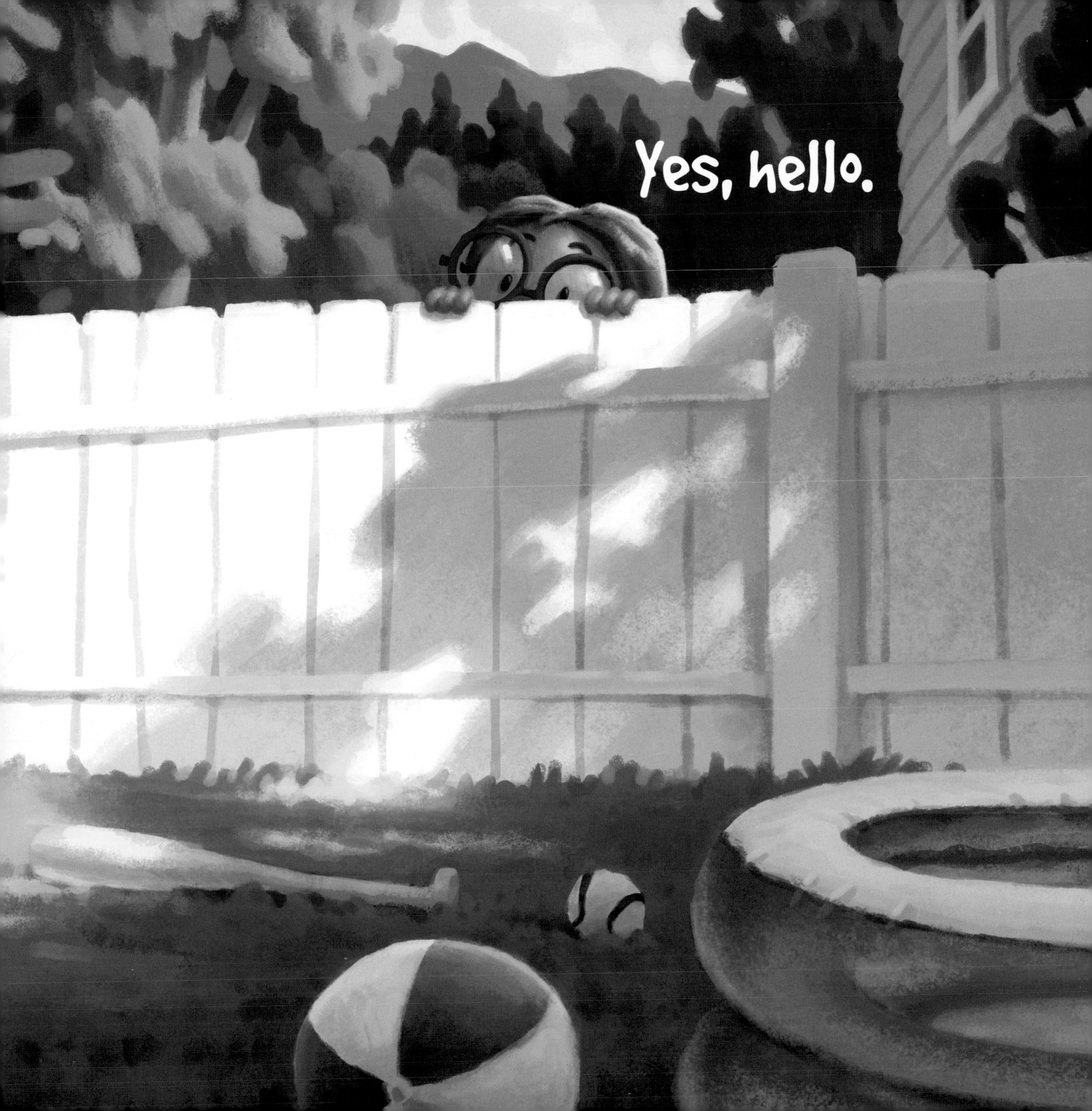
Yes, hello.

Ninjas hop. Ninjas chop.

Ninjas love to belly flop.

But when a ninja's not alone

he promptly turns as still as stone.

He will not speak. He will not blink.

He will not sip a juicy drink.

A neighbor girl can leap and spin
to try to make a ninja grin.

But once she's finished in the air,
the ninja is no longer there.

He vanished like a northern wind,
too shy to make a brand-new friend!

He'd rather dance with fireflies

or listen to a pirate's lies

or leap around a thundercloud—

all to avoid a ninja crowd.

Maybe ninjas are afraid
to share the world that they have made.

No . . . that can't be it!

Ninjas are the best at all they do!

There should be more, not just a few.

You might be scared of someone new,

but danger is more fun with two!

Hello, ninja.

When two ninjas stick together

there is no storm they cannot weather

beneath the moon, beneath the sun,

with laughs and kicks and ninja fun.

For Grace, who believed.
—N.D.W.

For Danielle, my ninja queen.
—F.D.